CRANKEE DOODLE

by Tom Angleberger ✳ Pictures by Cece Bell

CLARION BOOKS • Houghton Mifflin Harcourt • Boston   New York

Clarion Books, 215 Park Avenue South, New York, New York 10003

Text copyright © 2013 by Tom Angleberger ★ Illustrations copyright © 2013 by Cece Bell

Clarion Books is an imprint of Houghton Mifflin Harcourt Publishing Company. ★ www.hmhbooks.com

The text in this book was hand-lettered by Cece Bell. ★ The illustrations were done in gouache.

Library of Congress Cataloging-in-Publication Data
Angleberger, Tom.
Crankee Doodle / by Tom Angleberger ; illustrations by Cece Bell.
p. cm.
Summary: A pony tries to convince his cranky owner to take a ride into town.
Includes notes about the song "Yankee Doodle."
ISBN 978-0-547-81854-2 (hardcover)
[1. Ponies—Fiction. 2. Mood (Psychology)—Fiction.
3. Humorous stories.] I. Bell, Cece, ill. II. Title.
PZ7.A585Cr 2013
[E]—dc23   2012001346

Manufactured in China • SCP 10 9 8 7 6 5 4 3 2 • 4500430935

For Caryn Wiseman

A feather? For my hat? I'd look like a fool with a feather stuck in my hat. Everybody would laugh at me. In the name of General George Washington, why would I want to put a feather in my hat?

First of all, why would I want to call my hat macaroni? I don't want to call my hat anything! It's just a hat! Second of all, why would putting a feather in my hat turn it into macaroni? It would still be a hat, not macaroni! Look at this hat! Does it look almost like macaroni to you? I don't care how many feathers you put in it, it's still just a hat. And besides, I don't even like macaroni!

You could buy a new hat.
Confound it, Pony! Are you trying to drive me crazy? How can I make myself more clear? I do not want to go to town. I do not want a new hat. I do not want macaroni. I do not want a feather. I do not want any other clothing, any other pasta, or any other parts of a bird. I do not want anything that they have in town. Let them keep their town junk in town!

Even if I did want something from town—which I do not—town is just too far. I'm exhausted from standing here arguing with you all day! I DO NOT WANT TO GO TO TOWN, I WILL NOT GO TO TOWN, AND I CANNOT GO TO TOWN!!

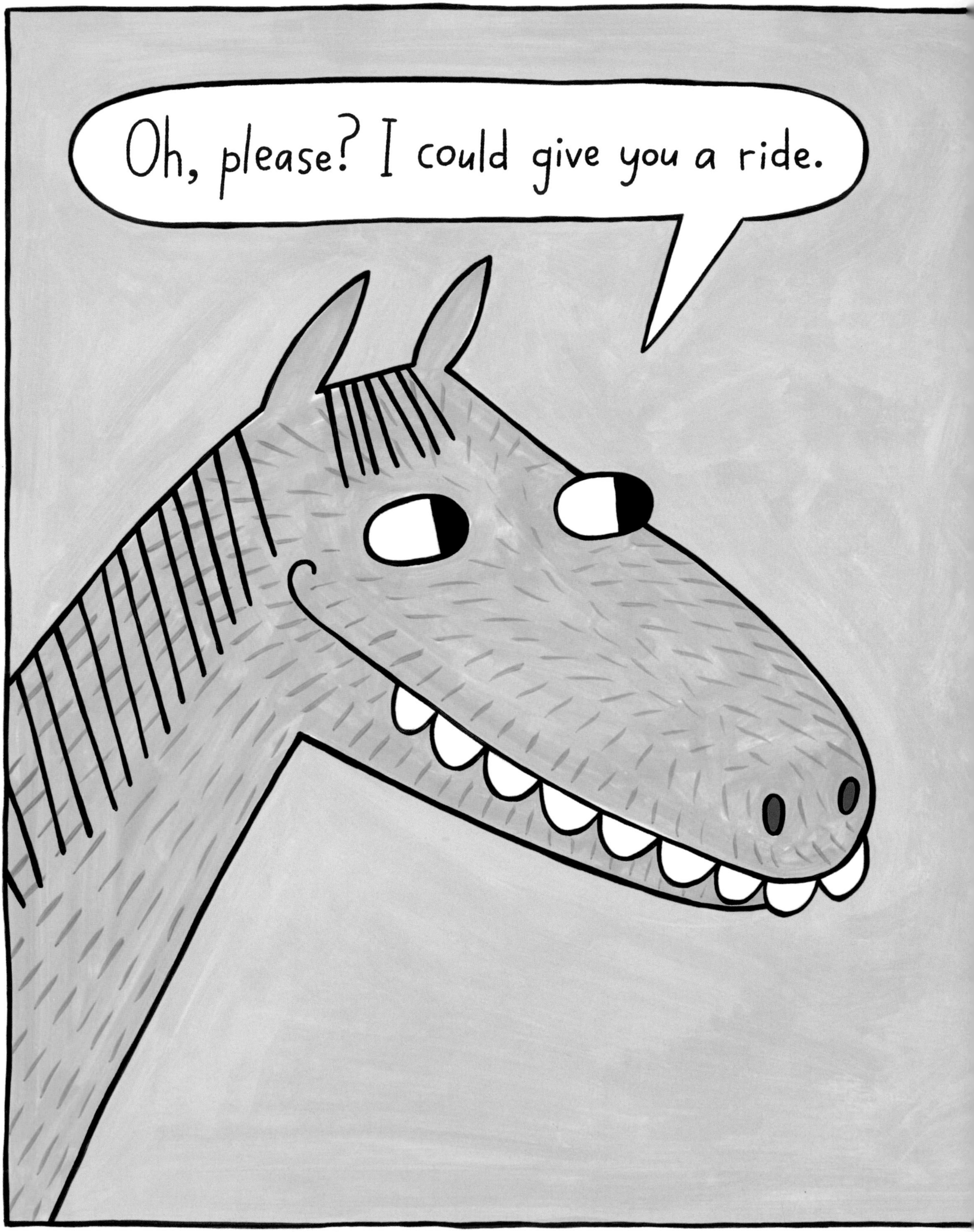
Oh, please? I could give you a ride.

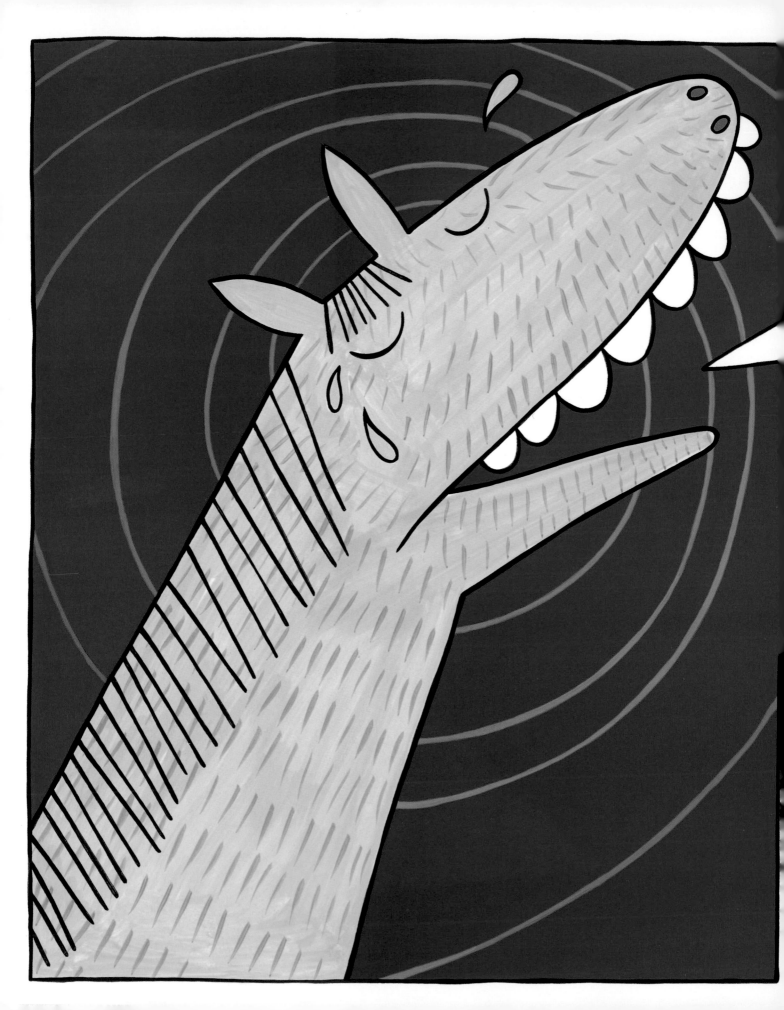

WHAT!? BOO HOO HOO! How could you be so cruel? I can't help the way I smell. SNIFFLE! I smell like a pony. This is the way ponies are supposed to smell. And, HEY! Aren't YOU the one who is supposed to give me a bath? But nooooo—SOB—you're always "too busy." You'd rather just complain all the time! SNIFF, SOB, SNORT!

Gee whiz.

All right, all right. We can go to town.

The End

Oh, my golly, the story behind the real song "Yankee Doodle" is just so fabulously exciting! It all started over 200 years ago—WOW!—before America had won the Revolutionary War and become a free country. It was so long ago that now no one knows who actually wrote the song. It may have been an Englishman who was making fun of the Americans, or it may have been an American colonist with a crazy sense of humor. First they would sing: "Yankee Doodle went to town, a-riding on a pony." (That's me! I'm a pony!) You know, back then they didn't have cars, so the fastest way to get to town was on a horse or pony. (That's me! I'm fast!) Then they would sing: "Stuck a feather in his hat, and called it macaroni." Macaroni really did mean "fancy," but I think the real reason they said it is because it rhymes with "pony." (That's me! I rhyme!) So when you put it all together, it's really fun to sing. In fact, I'll sing it RIGHT NOW! ♪ YANKEE DOODLE WENT TO TOWN, A-RIDING ON A PONY! STUCK A FEATHER IN HIS HAT AND CALLED IT MACARONI! YANKEE DOODLE KEEP IT UP!...

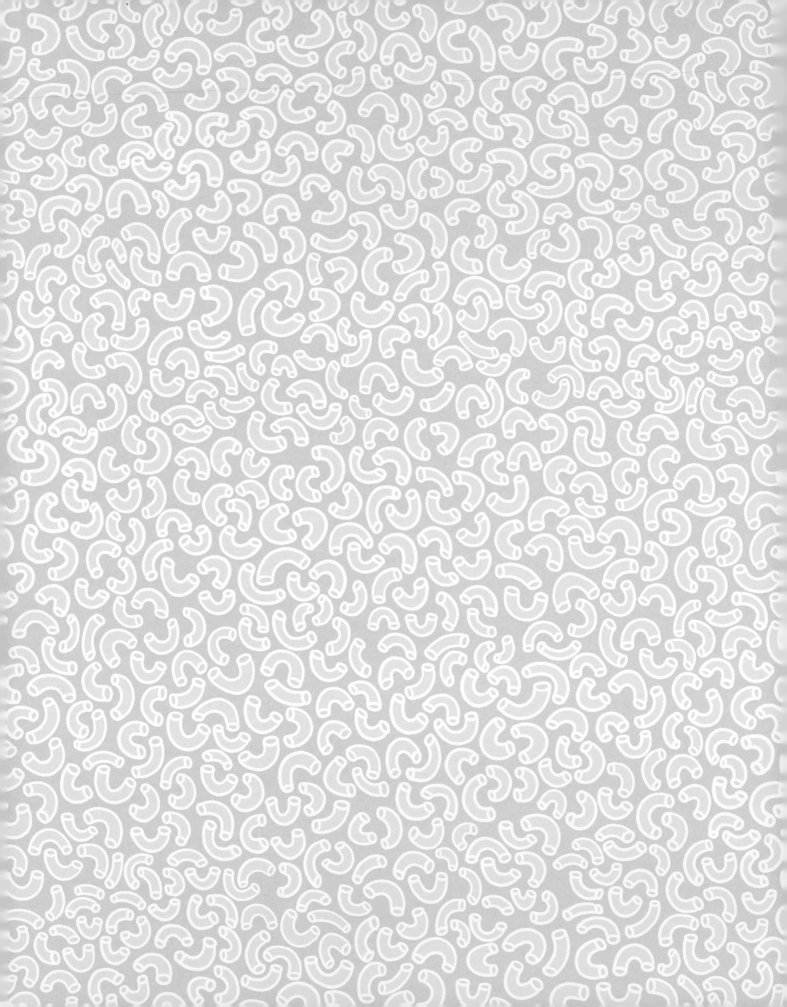